ROAN

LEGENETICS
THE RESEARCH FILES

BOOK 1

ALI LUCIA SKY

kbear ♡

this is coming

irl.

ali

BLURB

Tropes include:
- Fated Mates
- He Falls First
- Forced Proximity
- Research Experiments
- Demons & Devils
- Discovering Other Worlds

Blurb:

Roan Thibodault comes from a long line of Incubi and Succubi who understand the traditions of the demon breeds. Since they were children, he has understood that Winifred (Freddie) Marten is his Tether. Freddie has always been his, despite the fact that she's never given him the time of day or tried to understand the implications of his possessiveness or comments.

When the perfect opportunity arises to prove to her once and for all that they are made for one another, Roan is excited that she's agreed to get on board. But when Legenetics, a shady research conglomerate, takes over their lives and starts playing with what fate had planned for them, it becomes a nightmare for both.

ROAN

© 2024 by Ali Lucia Sky

This book is a work of fiction. Names, characters, places, and incidents reside solely in the mind of the author's imagination or are used in a fictional manner. Any resemblance to any person, living or dead, is purely coincidental.

Cover Designer: Artscandare
Editor: Bri Lind | BML Editing Services
Proofreader: Kalie Gerwig | Good Girl Author Services
Format: Kalie Gerwig | Good Girl Author Services

For permission to reproduce any of this novel, please contact Ali Lucia Sky at theskywriteshere@gmail.com

❀ Created with Vellum

CONTENT WARNING

This book includes *sexual situations* about sexual manipulation and sexual experimentation by 'scientists'. *Sexual proclivities and kinks* such as voyeurism, exhibitionism, somnophilia, and praise. *Discussions* regarding parental death, suicide ideation, and mental health issues.

ROAN PLAYLIST

- On The Outside – Charlotte Sands & Point North
- Maybe You're The Problem – Ava Max
- TYPECAST – Elio
- Gasoline – Cyan Kicks
- HSYEH – Dutch Melrose
- do you really want to hurt me – Nessa Barrett
- Flawless – The Neighbourhood
- bad idea, right? -- Olivia Rodrigo
- Suffocate – Kayzo, Bad Omens
- Beautiful Things – Benson Boone

To my demons,

Keep trying to kill me, and I will keep writing about you.

Love,
Ali

"Winifred Marten?" a deep voice from the other end of the hall calls. Like a Jack-in-the-Box, I pop up from my seat. I tug the AirPod out of my left ear and put an end to Charlotte Sands and Point North's song "On The Outside" just in time to hear my name called a second time. "Winifred, Winifred Marten!"

So much for not making the wrong impression with Professor Green. I need this work-study. I want to afford the creature comforts of life, like rent and food.

I make it to Professor Green's office and trip over the carpet trim strip, stumbling in through the door. I'm ready to apologize profusely for my awkward clumsiness, only to find that my advisor isn't there. Instead, the man sitting there is barely older than me and is, unfortunately, very familiar.

"Freddie Betty! Are you falling at my feet?" Roan Thibodault jeers.

I turn to leave, watching my step this time.

"Don't run. Don't you want to work as a glorified paper carrier in this department?" my childhood nemesis teases.

He's not only a pest but also one of those pesky Incubi that humans aren't supposed to know about. I probably wouldn't, but I grew up around the Thibodaults, Renaults, and Coulliards. They're all demons. Obnoxious Incubi with large egos and bank accounts.

Before my mom died, she and my aunt cleaned their fancy-pants houses. My aunt and the Couillards' nounou, Anaïs–Aris and Alex's nanny, have been longtime companions.

I don't know why the three families have always been superior and insufferable in my book. Maybe it's because they are well-established in society. Or it could be that they have those cocky French surnames. Whatever it is, Roan has always been the worst of the alphaholes. He's tortured me since birth. There are photos of him with his arms around my fat baby body professing ownership like I'm a Bumblebee Transformer someone will take away.

"Why are you here?" I ask him with narrowed eyes.

He shrugs and looks around. "Isn't it obvious? This is my job. I'm Professor Green's TA this year. Alyssa Chambers shuffled along last semester, and Etienne Sr. pulled some strings. Now, sit down on my lap and please me... while you call me boss, Freddie Betty."

"You're an idiot. I will be working for the department, not you, Roan. Not even Professor Green. He's my advisor. What I need from him is his signature. You can't do that for him as his TA." I back away and shake my head. "I don't even think I asked the right question, tho–"

He bites his lip and tilts his head to look around me. "You rarely do."

I ignore his rude comment and handsome face, which I want to make bleed with the tome of Collected Poe Works on Professor Green's desk. "Why, Roan? Why are you here right now?"

"I saw your name on his schedule. When he was called away, I volunteered to wait here for you. I promised you would be in good hands. I would always handle you gently and reverentially, Freddie. Well, at least our first time. Remember our first kiss? Ninth grade? Seven Minutes in Heaven? Best seven minutes of my life. Changed your world, right?"

Rolling my eyes, I turn to leave and bump into yet another body. "Sorry," I murmur, moving to scoot around them, but the person chuckles. From behind me, I hear an echoing sound.

"Don't leave now. This is my favorite part." Etienne Renault says. I look up to find another alphahole has joined us. He grins and continues, "We are seconds away from Roan, pulling your pretty turquoise braids and pissing on your leg because you're his clueless mate. You will say something unflattering about his intelligence, and I will take two steps back so he doesn't ruin my handsome face when you make him all insecure."

I raise my brow, tired of his bullcrap teasing. "Why are you here? Is it a dickhead convention?"

"Ms. Marten, I can assure you that it is not, in fact, a dickhead convention." Professor Green says, pushing around Etienne, causing me to close my eyes and hope the ground will open up and suck me into the fiery pits of Hell. When Green's back is turned, I stomp on Etienne's foot, which brings a growl from Roan.

Everyone freezes for a moment. Then there seems to be a sudden snap to attention, and I find Roan gently leading me to the only chair, leaving both him and Etienne to stand behind me like sentinels.

Green looks up and gives him an exasperated look. "Roan... you're not... she's not... does she even know what...?" My advisor stumbles over his words as he attempts to say nothing while getting the point across.

Roan places his hand on my shoulder and plays with my hair for half a second before I tug away from him and smack his fingers. Then he grabs my hand and kisses my knuckles, which sends butterflies to my belly.

"Freddie and I grew up together. She knows that all of us are Incubi. Her family promised her to me when they found out she was mine. It's all good that I'm here while you talk to her. Offer her the research. She can do it. Right, Freddie Betty?"

"Roan! Stop calling me Freddie Betty!" I growl out. "I hate it, and you know that."

He's annoyed me with the nickname since we were five and six. He called me Freddie Betty and followed me around, telling everyone I was his mate. When I demanded he explain it, he told me that it meant I was his. Nothing more, nothing less. It was an unmutable truth to Roan Thibodault.

"Okay, babe. No more Freddie Betty." His hand creeps under my curly-dyed locks to massage my nape. I relax and sigh. I try not to like it because it's Roan who's doing it to me.

Etienne hums thoughtfully. "Should I call you babe, too?"

"Professor? Would you please tell me why these two are still here?" I ask.

He nods. "Yes, let's get this back to the reason we are here. Ms. Marten–"

"Please, call me Freddie," I interrupt.

"Freddie, I realize you have a work-study allowance

through financial aid. However, it only allows you eight hours a week at a terribly low wage. When you expressed your need for this job, you told me you needed the money for living expenses because your scholarship didn't cover room and board. I'd like to offer you a paid position working with these two, plus Aris and Alexandre. There are also three other research candidates who are all women."

"Research candidates? What research does the Lit department do that you would pay me for?" I glance up at Roan to find him looking down at me. I then notice my hand in his, and he's been soothingly caressing his thumb over my knuckles.

"It's an outside group, babe. Legenetics. They are concentrating their study on pairs. The eight of us together would be the subjects for six weeks. We'd still be able to go to class and have a life outside of the requirements. That's how they explained it to us. I believe it's safe, or I wouldn't suggest it." Roan's expression is serious. For once, he's appealing to me as an adult and not needling me like a child.

"Freddie, it's safe. I can also promise you that the work-study will be yours as long as you are a candidate and you qualify."

I nod, looking from Roan to Professor Green. Inhaling, I lean into Roan as he gently combs his finger through my hair, and I finally notice that he's undone my braid. I don't get how he can both aggravate and settle me like no other. He's a complete ass.

"So, it's not contingent?" I finally ask.

Professor Green shakes his head slowly. "I swear it, but I urge you to take the research position. You will only benefit by being involved."

Etienne snorts. "You will benefit from Roan's dick and the rent-free situation that comes with the study."

I roll my eyes. "Okay. I'm done."

"I promise, Freddie. We will not be forced to do anything that will make you uncomfortable. Etienne's just being an asshole," Roan growls.

Etienne laughs. "Roan Thibodault is promising something, so mote it be! Fate wouldn't dare anger the Thibodault prince."

"Fuck off, Renault." Roan tries to block me as I stand. He gathers me in his arms, and for a second, I relax and allow him to comfort me before my sense kicks in.

"Let me go." I push him away and find Green holding out a signed document in my direction. I grab it and find it to be my work-study approval. I smile and nod at him. "Thank you. I will consider the other thing."

Roan arrogantly speaks up for me, "She accepts."

I shake my head. "I considered it. I have to decline because I can't take more of these two clowns in my life," I throw over my shoulder as I get to the door.

Green exhales, and it's so loud I stop and look at him to see what he'll say. He is giving Roan a flat look, but then his eyes swing to Etienne. "You better treat yours with more care."

Etienne smirks. "He's known she's his since they shared baby bottles. He needs to stop handling her with kid gloves and Claim her."

Roan moves my way as if protecting me from Etienne's words. "I know Freddie as well as I know myself; she's perfect. You haven't met yours yet. You'll get it one day." He turns to me and surprises me with a soft kiss on the corner of my lips, which sends a rush to every part of my body.

I push him away. "Roan, has anyone other than me ever

told you that you go too far and are the King of the Morons?"

He snorts and does it again, confusing me when I lean into him. "Baby, that fact makes you the Queen of them. I'll see you at Rammey's tonight. All of us research subjects are meeting there."

"Not going." I wave, walking away. "Oh, and I'm not going to be part of the Legion–whatever thing. Stop acting like I said yes."

"Legenetics. Legion is something else altogether, Freddie Betty. Don't make me come for you," Roan warns.

I give him the finger as I trip over the carpet trim again and head to my statistics class.

TWO

T stick my key in the lock of the place I'm staying, only to find the door is already open. I rent a room in this townhouse with three other people. I moved here two weeks ago at the start of the semester, and it's clear as crystal that I don't fit in with my roommates.

Really! Should there be a party on a Thursday night? It's the sixth one since I got here, and I hate it. No one needs to party *this* much.

My shoulders shake in misery. I'm so exhausted I could cry.

I'm carrying eighteen units and started work-study two days ago. When I'm not in class, I'm studying in the library or at the Lit Department. I can't stand it in this apartment. These people have no respect for me, my time, or my wishes.

I live with Christian and Seph, who play video games and watch an ungodly amount of sports at a ridiculous volume. They are very passionate about it, very loud, and they don't seem to sleep.

Then there is Sherré. She must be a sex addict. She is

never alone, never quiet, never kind enough to consider my room is next to her when she is being a 'good girl' and spanked or whatever else she does.

Tonight's party is soul-sucking. Ironically, "Maybe You're The Problem" by Ava Max is playing.

"Fred! Come here and have a drink with us!" Christian grabs my arm and pulls me away from the direction of my room. I try to shake him off, but he's leeched himself to me, and I can't shake him.

Sherré pops up from behind him with a blunt in her hand. She holds it out to me. I shake my head, and she extends her hand as if she insists. "Take a hit. You're going to need it. I'm so sorry about your room. We'll figure it out tomorrow. You can sleep at a friend's tonight, right?"

I widen my eyes at the news that shit is fucked up in my room. My *locked* room? How? I look from Sherré to Christian for further explanation, but it doesn't come from them. Seph slides up to the three of us with four shots. "It's not going to work out, Freddie. We'll refund you this month's rent and a few Benjamins for damages to your shit. But things got real in there tonight. Come back tomorrow."

He then hands me one. "To new beginnings."

"What are you talking about?" I shove the shot in Christian's hand and turn to head to my room. The lock lays broken and mangled on the floor. People sit everywhere on my bed, dresser, and floor. All my belongings are strewn about the place, and my heart flutters and turns over when I see the broken cremation glass orb that was blown with my mother's ashes in it.

"Get out!" I scream, gathering all the pieces I can find of it.

My fury is met with laughter. Some stoned asshole

mimics me. "You get out!" He chuckles until he falls over. Clearly, he doesn't take me seriously at all.

I dig for a tote bag, pull my backpack off, and search for anything that looks dear to my heart that isn't ruined. A photo of my mom, Aunt Dawn, and I at the Renault's. Another of those annoying Incubi boys and me as kids in a broken frame. A fractured ceramic goat my aunt got me when we did goat yoga after my mom died.

Then I can't find more because my tears are blinding me. I stumble out of the room. Some girl cackles at me and grabs my hand and starts dancing with me. "Typecast" by Elio is blaring, and I actually like this song. I shake my head, hoping PTSD won't ruin it for me.

Pushing past her, I make it to the door and outside so I can call the person most likely to know what to do in this situation, my Aunt Dawn.

"Hello, Freddie-baby. What's wrong?" she answers the phone on the second ring.

I titter, slightly hysterically, sounding unhinged. "Oh, Aunt Dawn. How do you know something is wrong?"

"Baby, it's eleven-thirty at night. You wouldn't call at this time of night if it weren't dire. Tell me what's wrong." She sounds calm and soothing. Truth is, she and my mom sound so similar that it pains me to talk to her on the phone.

I sit down hard on the curb and launch into the story, ending it with, "They ruined everything. What am I supposed to do now? I can't make it to the public bus before it stops running, and the campus ones stop at ten. Can you come get me?"

"Don't worry. I've sent someone who is closer and ready to fight this battle. Hang tight and stay on the phone." I can hear her walking around her house. "Thanks for leaning on me. You try to do too much by yourself. Oh! Roan just texted me. He is going to be there in five minutes,"

"Aunt Dawn! Please tell me you didn't call Roan and his flying monkeys! I can't stand it when he's my Nutless in Shining Armor."

She laughs. "Oh, but I did. You know what he is to you. Anaïs and I talk about it all the time. You and he are fated. That boy is your Shining White Knight for life. Trust him, Freddie. Trust him with your life."

Anaïs is the Couillard's nounou, who has never retired. She is a beloved family member and my Aunt Dawn's best friend.

A flashy sports car pulls up, and the front doors open as I attempt to look into the tinted windows. I sigh. "The cavalry arrived. You didn't tell me he was bringing everyone."

"Call me in the morning, Freddie." My Aunt makes me vow to her that I will before I hang up.

Roan reaches me just as I drop the hand holding my phone. "They threw you out, Freddie? Please tell me that I read your aunt's text wrong." I feel the tears fill my eyes again, and he shakes his head and pulls me close in a tight embrace. "No one treats my mate like shit and survives."

I look up in time to see his eyes black with the tell-tale red ring. He's going to cause trouble, and I want it to happen. I don't know if that makes me a bad person, but I'm so hurt and angry.

Alexandre Coulliard and his brother Aristade stand back from us as Roan comforts me until I break away from him. Alex comes close enough to take my bags and gently puts them in the trunk of his Lexus RC 350 F Sport.

"Well, what are we waiting for? Let's go fuck some shit

up." Alex smirks, and his eyes flash black too. All demons have these freaky black eyes with red irises.

"We don't have to go back in. There's no point. They destroyed everything." I sniffle, the tears falling again. Roan pulls me to him and massages the back of my head with his large hand.

Alex chuckles. "Freddie, that's more reason, not less." He leads, and Roan follows. He places me behind him, and Aristade brings up the back.

Aris taps my shoulder. "Etienne is back at the research house. He didn't want to leave the girls alone. Otherwise, he'd be here too."

"That isn't necessary," I reiterate.

When we enter, Christian and Seph see us instantly and make it our way. "Fred, I already told you. It would be better if you came back tomorrow. If there is anything left, you can grab it then. I'll have your money then, too."

I snort, and Roan pulls me by my hand to his side.

Sherré comes over, and she's dancing and singing, "'Cos you're burning your house down. The lights won't guide you home."

"Nice, bitchface," Alex says. He then pushes past them and finds the device that is playing music and tears it out of the wall. Raising his voice, he yells, "Party at Zeta. Tell them Alexandre Coulliard sent you. If you are extra cool, stay chill, and you don't make my friend cry more, I'll get you tickets to see my brother's band. Maybe you've heard of them? Grimm Fables."

The house starts to clear out. Christian, Seph, and Sherré look upset, which stirs an ugly part inside me that gains joy from their distress.

Sherré suddenly notices Aris standing with me and

makes eyes at him, causing him to snort. "You're joking, right?" He shakes his head. "Not interested."

"What are you a racist?" She narrows her eyes on him.

"It's not a black or white thing. It's that you hurt my friend. You did her dirty. We aren't going to be good." Aris takes a step in front of me when Sherré moves our way.

As if seeing that the three guys aren't willing to sell me out for any cheap good time, she flicks her weave over her shoulder and grabs Christian's arm. I watch her drag him to the couch and straddle him.

Roan eyeballs Seph. "Tomorrow morning, I'm going to own this place. You'll have a fifteen-day notice to get the fuck out. All of you."

"You can't do that!" Seph cries.

Roan chuckles. "I'm a Thibodault. I already own half the town. What's another property?"

Aristade bumps my shoulder. "What room is yours, Fred? Lead me."

Seph sneers. "She doesn't have one."

"Don't make it worse for yourself, asshole," Roan warns.

Aristade and I walk to my trashed bedroom, and his swiftly drawn breath tells me that it's as bad in his eyes as it is in mine. I look for something, anything, to salvage in the catastrophe.

Aris grabs my hand and leads me back to the door we entered through. "I'll have your aunt and nounou come out tomorrow. Tonight, come back to the research house with us. As a matter of fact, accept the position. I think you know as well as I do that you have no other options now."

"I can't stay with you," I say absently. "I don't understand what they are looking for. Roan's words that this research thing is safe isn't enough."

He smiles sadly at me. "Take my word, then. The way they sell it, it sounds straightforward enough. Four women, four men. They are looking to see how couples respond to one another under duress- in your case, an Incubus and a human. The housing comes with it, which would be perfect for you. All our food is covered. We are four days into this, and your boy has refused every partner while waiting for you."

"Why has he refused?" I ask.

"They are trying to simulate a mated couple, and he's not mating anyone else the way they explained it. They test the hell out of us, pair us up, monitor us, and the rest of the time is ours."

"Can you be my partner?" I joke.

"No. Never," comes a quiet and definitive reply from behind me. I turn to find Roan there. "You're mine, Freddie Betty. I wish you'd stop running."

"I know. That is your go-to for all your barbarian behavior. I belong to you." I look around. It's not like I have a lot of options.

As a matter of fact, I have no options. None, except for joining this research project. I nod. "I'll go with you, but Roan, if you behave like a fucking dog and pee on my leg or cover me in your dog slobber trying to protect me as a chew toy, I will snip your plums and stuff them down your throat. Do you get me, you Neanderthal?"

"You know, there is a lot of proof that Neanderthals are what humans evolved from and that demons probably descended from a more advanced civilization," Alex says, joining us now from further down the corridor.

"So you're all aliens? I could have guessed that the first time Roan laid his lips on mine." I shrug. "It gave me this feeling..."

"Soaked panties?" Roan grins.

"A headache and the need to vomit," I counter.

Aris ignores us, looks around again, and types a message. "Nounou will be here in the morning. She will box up anything she can save and drop off your belongings at the Thibodault's for safekeeping.

I sigh. "Thanks, Aris."

Roan mocks me. *"Thanks, Aris. You came immediately to my rescue. You jumped into action and had to be talked off the ledge by your friends when you found out your mate was in danger."*

"Still don't understand what that means, and you only make fun of me when you explain it. I don't know what your babble is supposed to explain. I know I'm probably not your anything, and this research we will be part of will prove it." I inhale and shake my head. I'm so tired.

Roan moves in and grabs my hand, pulling me out of the mess with him. "You don't know what you are, Freddie Betty. But you're right. The research will finally prove it."

THREE

The entire ride over to the research house is tense. Roan holds my hand, and I keep wondering why I'm allowing it. Is it comfort? Do I feel comfort in being with my Nutless in Shining Armor, who rode to my rescue? Can't be. Roan is my nemesis; that fact will surely never change.

Alex pulls into the driveway of a Victorian monstrosity, which is not far from where my townhouse is located but on the other end of the campus. It's the wealthy neighborhood of East Bethany. As with all of the neighborhoods in this area, the location is mere blocks away from the food and bar mecca of Main Street.

"Alright, your mate is safe. I'm off to Rammy's for some beer and a blowjob." Alex waves, walks down the drive to the sidewalk, and disappears.

Aristade snorts. "He and Dominique are failing this experiment, on purpose."

I look up at the house. "Is staying here really covered?"

Roan closes the trunk and comes over with my two bags. "Sure is, Freddie Betty. Let's get you inside."

Aristade leads us in through the front door. "Hey! Where is everyone?"

"Kitchen!" a woman's voice replies.

Roan heads upstairs with my bags, and I follow Aristade.

Etienne sits next to someone I'm relatively acquainted with. She's also a demon. Abrielle Manne is drop-dead gorgeous, with strawberry blonde hair and Dutch braids. As if that's not enough, she's unbelievably kind. When she sees me, her eyes brighten, and a sincere smile welcomes me as she jumps down from her stool and comes to me for a hug.

"Roan was miserable as we waited for you. I'm so glad you're finally here. But sorry to hear that shitty humans pushed you out of your home." She puts an arm around me. "Want food?"

Etienne shakes his head. "Abby, Roan can make her food if she's hungry."

"So can I, you heartless bastard. I am trying to make a friend. I know you don't know how to be one, but goodwill is the first step." She hip-checks him on the way to the refrigerator.

I can't help but smile. I'm going to like it here with Abrielle as one of the people in this cohort.

Aris takes a seat on the barstool next to Etienne. "Terralee? Is she here?"

"She and Dominique went to Rammy's." Etienne watches Abrielle, but I wouldn't say it was attraction. It seems more like a sibling-like concern. It further proves my supposition when he shakes his head and says, "Damn, Abby. You are holding the knife upside down. You're going to cut your finger off."

"Shut up." She looks over her shoulder and holds up the

knife in question to prove she's holding it correctly. "You are going to have to get a grip. I can make a sandwich."

"I just wish there was a cook here." Etienne makes a face and turns to Aris. "Her mom told me she'd kill me if she got so much as a hangnail."

"So, you aren't a couple?" I ask.

"God, no!" Abrielle says. "This is going to be a mess. We're cousins. We didn't realize they expected... *stuff*... until it was too late."

"What stuff do they expect?" I ask nervously.

Roan grabs my hand and pulls me into his arms. "Don't worry about it right now. You've had a shitty enough night. Just relax, eat your sandwich, and then we will chat."

Aris purses his lips. "Anyone want to watch a movie?"

I shake my head. "I have a nine a.m. class. It's already after midnight, and I'm going to be a bitch to wake up."

Abrielle hands me a plate with a ham and cheese sandwich piled high with lettuce, tomato, and red onion. "Head up to bed, but take this with you."

I smile at her. "Thanks."

Roan grabs it and kisses my temple. "Let's go upstairs. You're about to have a moment of displeasure, and I want to get it over with so you can get some sleep."

When we make it to the room, I look around. There is a queen-sized bed and a ton of equipment that looks like video monitors, heart and blood pressure machines, and a table with tubes for blood drawing.

"What in God's name is all this, Roan?" I whisper.

He walks in and sets my food on the nightstand. "Worry about it tomorrow. For tonight, let's face the battle of the fact that we are going to be sharing a bed."

I look at him, eyes wide, and shake my head. "Why? This house must have ninety bedrooms."

"Freddie, I want you to eat your sandwich and pretend we are still kids. Remember us sharing beds and baths until we started first grade? This is just like that." He rubs his eyes tiredly.

"Really, Roan? You want me to remember a time when you wet the bed on a night like tonight?" I scoff.

He snorts a tired laugh. "That was you, baby."

"Was not!" I argue, lost to the tangent he's led me to.

He reaches back and pulls off his burgundy t-shirt, leaving his muscular chest on display. I look away so I don't check him out and embarrass myself.

The shirt hits me in the face. "You can sleep in that."

"In your dirty clothes?" I ask in disbelief.

"It's not dirty, I put it on to come get you." He unzips his jeans, and I do a janky pirouette to avoid seeing him in the buff.

Roan chuckles. "My life is complete with you in it, Freddie Betty."

I don't hear him cross the floor, but suddenly, his arms are around me as he lifts the shirt I'm wearing up from the waist. "Lift your arms, baby. You aren't wearing this shirt to bed; you smell like that shithouse you rented."

I reach up, pull the neck up, and take a sniff. It stinks like cigarette and weed smoke. I immediately lift my arms with his shirt in my wadded up in my right hand. When he unclasps my bra, I gasp. "Roan Beaumont Thibodault! What in all that's holy!?"

"Can't be comfortable, Freddie Betty Marten. Has to come off." Next, he grabs the shirt and pulls it down my arms. I smell his intoxicating scent as it falls over my face to rest on my shoulders. The shirt is too large and slips off one side.

When I feel his lips press against my neck, I jump at the

sensation, only to turn to a seductive sucking, causing me to sigh. "What are you doing?" I whisper.

"Marking my mate," he whispers back.

Then he reaches under the shirt he put on me and unbuttons my jeans. A moment later, he pushes them down, kneeling behind me to get my feet out of them. He leaves a sucking kiss behind one knee and then the other thigh.

"Roan," I whimper, my voice is weak, and I'm so confused.

He leads me to the bed. "The bathroom is down the hall. Do you want to use it before or after you eat, baby?"

Raising my eyes to meet his, I open my mouth, embarrassed to hear my voice break when I answer. "Eat."

"I'm going to go brush my teeth then." He bends down and leaves a soft kiss on my lips.

I barely taste the sandwich that Abrielle made for me, confusion filling my head. I can't figure out how Roan is seducing me just by being in the same room after years and years of me discounting him. I've read tons of paranormal romance and can't help but wonder if I'm going through some sort of heat? Maybe the Incubus has been going light on me all my life, and now he's using magical powers against me.

My head hits the pillow. I'm so tired. I close my eyes and then laugh hysterically for a few seconds. "Please, please, don't tell me that after all this time, it's happening to me because the words he constantly repeats about me being his mate actually mean something," I whisper to myself.

FOUR

I wake up cuddled up next to Roan, and I barely slip out of our shared bed before there is a knock on the bedroom door. I pull it open and look over my shoulder to be sure he's still asleep. Abrielle is standing there with a hopeful smile on her lips.

"Want to head to campus together? We can get some coffee on the way." Abrielle glances at my top, and I look down, remembering I'm wearing Roan's shirt.

"Oh! We didn't—I-I mean, he gave me... We s-s-slept together, but we didn't d-do anything," I stutter and trip over my words.

Abrielle shakes her head and holds up both hands. "I wasn't going to say anything."

"Let me get some clothes on, and I will be right out," I say, closing the door in her face, rudely.

From the bed, rich, decadent chuckles come from the yummy Incubus I want to smother with a pillow.

"Shut up, Roan." I pull on the jeans I wore yesterday and reach for my Skechers. Knowing my dire clothing situation, I steal one of Roan's sweaters and pull it on.

23

His eyes watch me, and he smiles happily as I pull books out of my bag and search for what I want to bring. "Come back to bed, Freddie. Let's snuggle."

"As if!?" I snort. I can't find my statistics workbook, but I will mention it to Aunt Dawn and see if she and Anaïs can find it at the apartment.

As I stand, Roan rolls out of bed, catches me around the waist, and holds me tightly. "I'm going to meet you after your morning classes," he says.

"We'll see. I still have work-study," I say, trying to pull away from him. Roan kisses my throat, moves to the door, and opens it for me. The act confuses me, and I inhale the nonsense, thinking exhaling will make it come together. But instead, I get a slap on the ass.

"Dickhead," I say under my breath as I walk out.

"Freddie Betty, I'll be giving you more than the head soon," he replies.

Abrielle is downstairs waiting for me in the kitchen. Dominique Finch is with her, and I nearly run back to the bedroom. Dom is a tall, fit woman who is on the school dance team. She's normally giving off RBF and hooking up with guys who have a lot of money.

She shakes her head and sips her dalgona coffee. "I want to trade in Alex for Roan or Aris. Alexandre is a real balloon knot. I can't stand him."

"At least you aren't expected to hook up with your cousin. Legenetics is fucked up." Abrielle looks like she is sickened by her situation with Etienne, and I don't understand completely what is going on, but I do understand the gist of it. It makes *me* feel uncomfortable, and I'm matched with Roan.

"Knock, knock?" a woman's voice sounds a moment

before a group of people enter the kitchen from the other door.

"Woohoo! It's Dr. Kevorkian and his helpers," Dominique says, rolling her eyes and spinning her finger around in a snarky expression of excitement.

A tall man standing behind everyone else smiles, his black demon eyes with their red iris not even human-looking as a courtesy. "Is that Roan's mate?" he asks.

Abrielle and Dominique turn around. Dominique shakes her head and turns back to address the demon and his entourage, disregarding my presence. "I still would like to change my partner for Ro or Aris. I doubt that Little Bo-Peep there is really his mate."

For some reason, it pisses me off that this woman wants Roan. I step into the room and surprise myself when I hear myself claim, "I'm Roan's. You and I haven't met. My name is Winifred Marten. You can call me Freddie."

The tall demon comes forward, smiling, as he extends his hand. "Benjamin Elliot. This is my research project. Let me introduce you to Thomasina Rivers and Claude Aoilux. They are the technicians for the experiments. I also have a monitor who will be here a little later; her name is Carney Willis."

"I'm unsure of what this is exactly. I'm here mainly because I have nowhere else to go. I don't know what you're doing here, beyond the fact that you have a lot of equipment in the room Roan and I stayed in last night and..." I wave my hand in Abrielle's way. "And you placed her with a family member."

Thomasina laughs. "That is not as awful as it sounds, I promise you."

I look at Abrielle, and we mirror one another as our

eyebrows raise. I'd like to find out how it's less awful at some point.

"We need to get some base evaluations on you this morning. You need to do some questionnaires as well. I can do swabs, blood, and a physical after all of that is complete." Thomasina nods as she speaks, and I watch her defer to Benjamin at the end of her list.

"Sounds good. Make sure she is covered from absences in her coursework," he replies.

"But I have to go to class," I argue.

"You can return to class later this week. Right now, the only thing you have to do is go to the lab with Thomasina." Benjamin gives me a small smile and nods. His dark eyes are starting to unnerve me.

I hear footsteps behind me. An arm comes around my shoulders, and I know it's Roan. "What's happening?"

"They are trying to get me to go with them rather than go to class!" I complain.

"For what reason?" Roan moves before me, blocking everyone from access to me.

Thomasina rubs her hands together gleefully. "It's time to see what makes your mate special."

I watch Roan shake his head, and his arm comes back to hold me in place. "I go where she goes."

"I'm going too," Abrielle throws in.

Benjamin cackles. "Good, I can see how you all are physically reacting to your new roommate."

This 'research project' commands all my time for days. Benjamin demands more and more of my class hours, and my coursework piles up. The only thing that this house is good for is finding quiet study nooks to get comfy in and lose myself in reading material.

Not that this moment is one of those moments as Dominique is blaring "HSYEH" by Dutch Melrose and shouting at Thomasina about the same thing she is always arguing with her regarding wanting Roan or Aristade.

"I am trading him in! Give me Roan. Fuck Alexandre, he's a pig. I'm not pretending anything with him. I'm not sleeping next to him when he's covered in perfume from hooking up with other girls! He is hardly keeping up with the rules of this research's guidelines. Yet, you don't let me leave this place without a babysitter!" She throws a shoe at Thomasina, and I shake my head and try not to laugh.

"Who is that?" Dominique screeches.

I figure I'm found, so I call out, "Just me!"

"Oh, of course. Freddie has made Roan into a golden retriever. Abrielle's told me all about you two. He's been your faithful puppy all his life. What a waste!" She throws the other shoe at me.

Roan walks in with a bowl of food as it flies in our general direction. "What the hell? Dominique, if that hits Fred, I will remove your throwing arm like the cheerleading Barbie you are."

"I'm on the dance team, demon," she scathes.

"Cheerleader is the same thing, human," he yells back as she stomps up the stairs.

"It really isn't," I argue.

"Doesn't matter." He sits next to me on the settee. "Scoot a little, baby. This is big enough for both of us."

I move my book bag, and as I'm in the process of sliding out of mermaid pose, Roan grabs my legs and draws them over his lap. "I brought you some food. Don't worry, I didn't cook it, so it's edible."

"Who made it?" I ask.

"Aris and Abby. We can trust them. They are the least fucked up of all of us." Roan brings a bite to my lips.

"I'll have you know that I'm not fucked up," I say, moving away from the fork.

"You have to eat, Freddie Betty," he huffs. It's an actual entitled huff that I've seen him give his mom's Yorkie when the doggo doesn't do its business when he takes it outside.

"Don't you dare huff at me, Thibodault," I warn. "I ate a late lunch, and I'm not very hungry. I need to read these chapters. I'm so behind in Western Civ. it's not funny. I've had to do all these stupid Legenetic sample studies this week, I've literally given them my blood, sweat, and tears."

Roan smirks and then laughs. "I see your blood, sweat, and tears and raise you sperm samples, both before and after being exposed to your pheromones. Let me tell you, after your pheromones, I gave more. Those were our children I sacrificed. Now eat this mac and cheese before I give up on feeding you, and I make you into my dinner."

I give him a dirty look, and he only grins at me. His eyes skate across my bare shoulder. "I like you in my clothes. You should wear nothing but my clothing all the time."

I shake my head and try to go back to my reading. Roan grabs my book, closes it, and tosses it on the floor. He sticks the fork in front of my face, and I lean forward and snatch the bite while narrowing my eyes on him.

"Good girl." He smirks.

"Shut up, Roan!" I go to grab the bowl, and he pulls it away from me.

"Nuh-uh, baby. Open up, you can take me." He grins at this dirty joke, and I push him away with my hand over his face.

"I really hate you, Ro," I mumble as he stuffs a mouthful of mac and cheese in my face.

He nods and stirs the bowl. "Did you read your email from Benjamin today?"

I shake my head. "I've been trying to do actual coursework."

"Our compatibility tests are in." Roan bites his lower lip. I watch his eyes flicker black. For some reason, the change sends warmth down my spine instead of the shiver Benjamin's dark eyes caused.

"What do the results say," I whisper.

Roan leans forward, and for some reason, I don't move away when he softly presses his lips to mine and sits back. He lifts the fork back to my mouth again, and I keep my eyes on him as he says, "It needlessly confirms what I've been telling you all our lives. You're my mate."

I move back, and some of the creamy cheese sauce drips on my lower lip. Before I can lick it off, Roan's thumb is there to wipe it clean. I watch as if under a spell as he brings his hand to his mouth and licks it off.

Looking into his eyes, the black and crimson are a red flag warning that I'm in over my head. "Explain it to me, Roan. You've said it so long. Make it make sense. It's just wonky demon hoopla right now."

"Hoopla? Is that a word from this century?" Roan teases.

I can't control my grin. "Actually, it's of French origin. It was the word of the day a few weeks ago, as well as some time in the last two centuries."

"You being my mate is a demon thing." He nods his head and holds another bite of food out to me. "Demons are particular, there is an old-world term for what you are to me; it's called a Tether. Most modern demons don't believe in it, or the idea was forgotten generations ago. Our families here are very traditional. Very ceremonial. Not only do we believe in it, we live it, we wait for our Tethers. If we don't find them, we choose to die alone."

I shake my head. Around a mouthful of noodles, I say, "What about Maxime Jr.?"

"Adopted and one hundred percent human. Noémie Couillard couldn't conceive when she first married the elder Maxime. They adopted Maxime, but a few years later, Alexandre came along, then Aristade. Maxime Jr. doesn't have the demon life rules applying to him. Being human is why he had such a rough patch with women. Humans just don't have the same fateful future awaiting them." He looks sad about that, and Roan's ability to empathize for his friend's brother touches my heart.

"But you have me?" I ask.

He nods and looks up. Leaning forward, he brushes his lips against mine. "I've been so good waiting for you, Freddie. I've waited, never crawling into your dreams, never searching your wants. More than anything, I want to spread you open and crawl inside you. I want to lay next to you while you sleep and feed for hours and days. I'm dying to finally live with you like we should have been living for years."

I feel like he's a mesmer, his words and tone hypnotizing me. I can't hold back the moan that is drawn out from somewhere deep inside. His eyes are pools of liquid ink and the red hot chilis that call to me. He rolls his forehead against mine and groans.

"I want you to know, this isn't what I thought we would experience here. There is nothing natural happening in this house between us, baby." He looks so sad. "I can only hope we get out of this together on the other end."

He kisses me again. It's sweet and feels like an apology. "No one but me will ever feel like that to you, Freddie."

"Mr. Boner is trying to seduce you. How bittersweet," Dominique interrupts, coming down the stairs. "Don't believe any shit these assholes say, Fred. I am calling a squad meeting in the kitchen."

"Squad?" I echo, unsure of her meaning and off balance from the intimacy I was just sharing with Roan.

Roan stands and grunts, adjusting himself in his jeans. "Dominique is using cheerleader speak."

"Dance team, you freaking idiot," she grits out, grabbing the shoe she threw at me earlier and heading to the kitchen.

I tug Roan's arm. "You do know there is a difference, right?"

"Definitely," he laughs. "But she's such a mean heifer, I enjoy pissing her off."

With the empty bowl of mac and cheese in one hand, he interlaces my fingers with his with the other.

When we get to the kitchen, we find it's far from a small gathering of us house guests. Benjamin and Thomasina are there with my advisor, Professor Green and our Dean, Sebastian Oliver.

Confused by the collection of individuals, I feel my heart pound harder.

Benjamin wears a smug smile. "We are most pleased with four of our study subjects. The rest of you will stay here on an individual basis, for environmental reasons. Dean Oliver is here to assure you that this will be what you will be graded on this semester."

I turn to the Dean and feel my heart fall when his eyes turn black with that red flag ring. "The remainder of you will be foregoing your semester work and will get your pass on unit work based on how you carry yourself in this house. Your sole endeavor this semester is to let yourself be monitored while you mate, bond, and Claim your partner."

"Like fuck you will monitor my Claim." Roan shakes his head. "Call my father."

Benjamin laughs. "It's too late now, Mr. Thibodault. You are mine now."

CHAPTER
SIX

That night, I find myself standing in a frigid room with a moody and difficult Roan. His demeanor is cold and disinterested so soon after professing a dying need to be with me. I grab my clothes and sigh. "Roan, you need to unscrew yourself. This isn't going to get any easier. I'm going to go get dressed. It's freezing in here."

All afternoon Abrielle had Nessa Barrett's "do you really want to hurt me" playing in the house, and it's a total earworm. As I walk down the hall to our room, I run into Dominique's blasting "Flawless" by The Neighbourhood.

I walk into the room. "Augh, I'm going to have the most annoying song mix in my head tonight." I rub my hands up and down my arms and walk to the bed to get in on my side. "Do we have more blankets?"

"No, they want us to make each other warm, Freddie!" he says it like it should be obvious.

I look his way to find him giving the bed a dirty look. "What are we supposed to do?"

He grunts, lifting his chin to the filming equipment.

"We won't be doing anything natural with all that bullshit."

"I've not felt anything natural since I entered the door to this wonky world two weeks ago. As a matter of fact, natural left the boathouse with the ship whose cargo was common sense." I sigh.

Sucking his lower lip and inhaling, he shakes his head. "Sorry, Freddie. I shouldn't be taking this out on you. I'm mad because this has gone so far afield. I didn't know they could do this to us. I don't know how we are getting out of this. I'm responsible for trapping my Tether in a science prison. I'm an arrogant and irresponsible mate."

Roan reaches for the hem of his burgundy sweater, and even after all these nights of sleeping next to his bare skin, I turn away from looking at his flawless golden physique. This time, I awkwardly examine the equipment the research team brought into the room and set up. There is little room left other than the bed, which is their focus anyway.

I start looking in boxes and bins. When I come across one full of sex toys, I hold up a set of ears and butt plug tail. "Ro? What the hell would they want with this?"

He looks up, and his lips twitch. "At least they got something that is teal. It matches your hair and eyes, baby."

I toss it down, cringing. I get chill bumps.

"Want to try it?" He starts laughing.

"No! Abso-not!" I say, but something is in his eyes that makes me feel like a cornered animal. I take a step toward the door, and he shakes his head.

"Don't run, Freddie Betty. I will chase. If I chase you and catch you, and I *will* catch you, all my predator instincts will insist I Claim you." His voice is low, growing more and more guttural.

I take a few steps toward the door and then turn away from him.

"You are testing me, it's a bad idea." I don't hear him move, but suddenly, he's close enough to wrap his arms around me. I sag against him as he embraces me. I have to admit to myself that I love being in Roan's orbit. The scent of him, the way he knows how to read me. Right now, he knows that I want to run. I want him to chase me. But he knows what's good for me too.

He lifts my hair and pushes it over my shoulder. "I love that you went with a teal."

"The color is Aqua-Mermaid. It's aquamarine, my favorite color," I whisper.

"It matches your eyes, baby. That's *my* favorite color. Your eyes and the little storm of freckles in them have been the only thing I've looked for since I learned my colors." Roan kisses my cheeks just below each eye. He moves to take my lips, and I feel him smile before he trails kisses to just below my ear. "I think I'm going to love the pink of your pussy and the color of your nipples too."

"Roan!" I push him away, trying not to laugh and encourage more of his dirty talk. "I thought you were being romantic!"

"Thibodault's show romance by cunnilingus. Want me to seduce you as my ancestors have for generations?" He laughs. "We should start satisfying your pussy now. Its only got eighty or so more years of perfecting the act ahead of us. We don't want to put it off."

"What happens if I run?" I quietly ask.

"Don't run. Ask me anything if you are scared. But running from a predator is never a good choice. You're mine, and I'll always cherish you, but I'm dangerous if you try to run. I will follow and convince us both, and anyone else around us, that you are mine."

I nod, accepting his reason. "Can you tell me what the equipment does? There is so much more of it than before."

Roan runs his nose up my throat and scents me. I mirror him, and his natural musk spins my head. "I want more of you," I whisper.

He nods, but as if I didn't just divulge my desire, he pulls me to the video equipment. "I told Thomasina that nobody could sit in here and watch us. She, Claude, and Carney aren't welcome. They went over what they are asking me to do today. I didn't want to go forward with it, but they are going to pump a synthetic pheromone in here that mimics my scent to see how you react while we sleep.

"If you stay asleep, I'm going to feed, with your permission. I won't do it, not without your consent. I would never do anything to you while you sleep without your permission." He is so earnest.

I press my lips to his and nod. "Take care of me?" I beg.

"Of course, I didn't want to lay this on you while we are here, but I've loved you my entire life, Winifred Marten. I will always take care of you." He holds me like I'm something delicate and precious. I exhale, not realizing that I've been holding in some sort of stress breath for days. I just let it out, and Roan takes on some of the weight that was laying on my shoulders.

"I'm sorry, baby," he says softly. "I thought that this would be something easy and fun. I considered that the research might be a touch invasive or that it wouldn't offer so much in reimbursement. Whatever is going on here is more than I ever imagined. It's not what I would want you involved in."

"What were you signing up for, Roan?" I murmur, my eyes feel glued to his.

"More time with you. Maybe a chance for you to see me in a different way." He smiles sadly. "I wanted you to notice me."

I laugh, and it feels like the heavy spell that had come over us is momentarily broken. I move away from him and take a seat at the end of the bed. "Oh, I've been aware of you for a long time."

Thomasina knocks on the open door. "I hope you are getting comfortable."

I don't like her around Roan when he's missing so many articles of clothing. I stand, moving until I block him from her blatant perusing.

"What is happening tonight?" I ask.

"It's a simple viewing, with a little light stimulation. Dominique and Alexandre have a similar setup. We are going to let you get some sleep first. You're going to take these to relax." She holds out small oval pills from a round plastic case.

"What are these?" Roan asks carefully.

Thomasina leans back and grabs two bottles of water from Carney. "They are a Legenetics developed sedative. It works on demons and humans. There is no need to be concerned, it was tested for many years and has been used in our studies for over fifteen years."

Roan looks devastated as he looks from the pill to me, then back at Thomasina. "What if it's just me that takes it?"

"It's safe," Carney assures, and for some reason, I trust her more than Thomasina. I grab the pill from Roan's fist and drop it into my mouth, grabbing one of the waters to wash it down.

"Fuck, Freddie. I don't know what you just took." He

shakes his head and snatches the water from my grasp. "If this fucks up my mate, you are dead."

Thomasina smirks. "I'm scared."

Once they all leave, we make it under the covers. It takes about twenty minutes for the sedative to kick in, which I feel all at once.

"Ro? I feel fucked up," I whisper.

"Now you're worried, Freddie Betty?" He wraps his entire body around mine. "Tonight is the calm before the storm, my love. I will ensure that none of those monsters get to you."

"You're the only monster I'm worried about," I try to joke.

"I took the sedative too, I won't be eating you tonight either." He presses his lips to the spot just below my earlobe, and I shiver.

"Roan?" I whisper.

"Go to sleep," he says, rolling onto his back and pulling me over his chest, hitching my leg over his hip. "Let the sleep come, baby."

"What if they are wrong–" my words slur.

"No, no! You're mine. I know because it's as obvious as the nose on my face. If you would just give us a chance, you would know too," he murmurs.

I tuck my nose into the nook under his throat and catch his musky scent. It's comforting. I relax, but the cold of the room renders me incapable of being cozy. "Roan? Would you...?"

"Would I what?" He rubs his jaw and its bristling hairs against my shoulder. I feel something in my core heat but fail to reach my extremities.

"Would you be the big spoon?" I ask, trying to roll over. He helps me, and when he presses his hard cock against my soft backside, I relax and let myself feel for my alleged mate. If he's right, he's mine. All of him. Including this part of him that, at this moment, feels like puzzle pieces finally falling into place.

I sigh.

"What's wrong?" Roan asks, sounding sad.

"I think it's too late," I whisper. "There was never a chance to escape."

He chuckles. "If there was, it was briefly lived and a long time ago."

CHAPTER

SEVEN

Despite their ominous threats that something would happen during the night, nothing occurred to my knowledge. The morning is strange. I wake alone, and there is no sign of Roan.

When I make it downstairs, Aris informs me that he left early with Etienne to go to the gym for a workout. I go looking for Thomasina to ask her if this means I can leave the house to attend class.

She rolls her eyes my way and moves some of the monitoring equipment into Alex and Dominique's room. "You do remember filling out the waiver less than a week ago, remember? The contract said you would be available any time, day or night. You won't be available if you are on campus."

"But, Roan and Alex–" She doesn't allow me to go further.

"They are on their way back right now. They would have been told 'no' if they had asked before they left."

I look around at my prison system. "This is ridiculous, Thomasina. How is it that the Dean can just come in here and absolve us of our class commitments in the name of this science experiment?"

"Humans are always the last to grasp the notion that they are demon playthings. This campus, the entire town, is demon-run. Legenetics has donated a lot of money and time here, and the power they hold is immense. Your Dean is only one of the powerful demons that control the town. He can make up any rule he wants, and no little human is going to make enough waves to rock the boat in East Bethany. You might rile the other humans, but the demons can make all of you disappear for their trouble." She snaps her fingers. "Just that quickly."

"So what am I supposed to do while nothing else is happening?" I can't help but feel my anxiety race through my veins. "Am I allowed to talk to my aunt?"

"Not right now. We'll see if you can earn that privilege. For now, you can go see the other subjects." Her smile is smug, and I want to punch her in her annoying face.

I leave her humming, "bad idea right?" by Olivia Rodrigo, and I tromp down the stairs to the last place I had one of my Lit reading assignments. I grab the book and head to one of the nooks I like, and pull one of the lap blankets up over me. Classwork might be optional, but I can still read it for entertainment.

I repeatedly reach for my phone, only to remember that Benjamin had Claude collected them yesterday. I keep an ear open for the grandfather clock. When it chimes the full-hour sequence, I start to worry where Roan might have gone after the gym. My eyes grow heavy the further I read into Lucretius' *The Way Things Are*.

"Freddie, baby?" I hear Roan's voice. It's soft, and a delicate feather touch brushes my hair from my forehead.

I'm barely awake when I roll off the settee and into his

arms. I bury my nose in his chest and breathe him in. "Roan," I whimper.

He rubs my back. "Just so you know, they wired the house for video and sound while you slept this afternoon. I just got home, and they showed me you've been here for the last four hours. Let's get you some food and a nice long shower."

It doesn't escape my notice that Roan is treating me like I'm the only thing that means anything to him. In the kitchen, he ignores Etienne and Abrielle's polite questions about his day. He is tunneled into my care and concerned only for me. When we leave, he leads me to the bathroom and turns on the sink's faucet and the showerhead, rubbing his eyes as if that is where his stress is gathering.

Pulling me close to him, he whispers, "They shouldn't be able to hear us over all the water. Last night, they watched us. Tonight, they are pumping my scent into the room. I'm sorry, baby. It's going to strip away your ability to say yes or no. I need you to do that now. Tell me 'no,' and I will walk away right now. But my fear is Ben will bring someone else in. Fuck, I hate Legenetics and this experiment."

"I want you to be my partner in this. I trust you. We've been in this for two weeks. You've proven yourself to me. We go through this as one unit. Don't let them hurt me," I beg, terrified. They're demons, and I know it's possible. "Promise me you'll protect me, Roan?"

"This lifetime and the next, Freddie." He kisses me.

I know he means the kiss to be a promise, but I need more. I slip my hands under his shirt and push it up and over his head, trailing my lips over his pectoral muscles as they are exposed. "I want to touch you. I need your body against mine, Ro!"

For a moment, he looks conflicted. There is a war being waged in his eyes. Desire raging against the instinct to shelter me.

"Kiss me, please," I beg.

He takes my mouth in a desperate press, his tongue battling against mine. His hands work to undo my jeans and push them down. As soon as we are naked, Roan gently steers me into the falling water. He washes me, only lifting his head to caress another swathe of flesh. I expect it to be sexual, but it's more like he's removing the sin that this experiment is leaving on my skin.

"I worship you, little mate. I have loved you my entire life." His words are redolent of his upset.

"Are you okay, Roan?" I whisper into his throat as I press my wet body to his.

"Nope. No, baby. This shitbin of a situation is impossible. Everything inside me is telling me to pack you up and run. But now, I know they would find us and lock us up in a less friendly place for a longer time. The thing is... I don't think we have the power to get out of here in three more weeks. That terrifies me." He pushes my hair back from my face. "I'm going to live with the shame of what I've done to my mate for the rest of my life."

I feel an overwhelming urge to look out for him. A bubble of concern for his well-being that flies in the face of all the animosity I felt for him before we were locked together and had to fight the odds of Legenetics. Somehow, our minds have aligned in how we want to care for one another.

"I don't blame you. I agreed to this, Roan." I press my lips to his jaw.

"Because you had nowhere else to go!" he forcefully says and pivots to turn off the cooling shower water.

He steps out and grabs a towel to hand to me before wrapping one around himself. He shakes his head as if he's having a conversation with himself.

"I'm not mad that we're here together," I whisper.

He snorts. "But will you still feel that way tomorrow morning?"

There is a knock on the bathroom door. "I need to separate you both for a few hours," Thomasina loudly calls.

I open the door and look back at Roan to see his eyes are black with a warning in the red irises. "Separate us? Why?" he challenges Thomasina.

"It's only for a few hours. Say your farewells, and you'll be back together in three hours and..." She examines her watch. "Thirty-seven minutes."

"Why?" Roan asks again.

"We are going to observe you. And we are doing hormone levels on your mate." She gives him a snotty look. "Is that acceptable?"

I interrupt, "Since you ended my birth control, my hormones are going to be all over the place."

Roan freezes. "You did what?"

"We need pure results," the researcher says.

"We are college students, not ready to become parents," Roan bites out.

Thomasina laughs. "Let's hope neither of you are fertile. But also, don't worry, any children that are born of this study will be ours."

I step back, and Roan moves in front of me. I place my hand over my abdomen protectively. Nothing is in there yet, but I would never let them have a part of Roan and me. Roan growls, and it sounds like an animal.

"Let's go," Thomasina says as if she didn't just threaten our future. Neither of us moves.

Her walkie-talkie goes off, and a tinny-sounding Benjamin comes across the speaker. "What's the hold-up?"

Thomasina looks at the two of us. "The Mister and Missus are being difficult. Probably sexual tension. Won't be a problem after tonight."

Ben's laughter comes from the device. "Tell Thibodault to hurry up. He has a lot to lose here if he doesn't give us what we want."

Not understanding that comment, I watch him reluctantly step forward. "Can I at least get some clothing on?" He narrows his demon eyes on Thomasina, and she flashes her demon eyes back. I hardly ever see her flaunt her demon traits.

"Ben is going to make you do tests that require you to drop your trousers anyway. So why bother?" She smirks, and I want to beat her with something heavy and deadly. When she turns away, I surreptitiously look down at her backside. I know she's the devil, I'm just trying to see if she has an arrow tail showing.

"So, now that your mate's gone, let me tell you a little bit of what will happen tonight. It's going to be so exciting..."

CHAPTER
EIGHT

ours later, I was swabbed and traumatized after they took blood, saliva, sweat and vaginal samples. I feel violated. I head back to the shower for the hottest and coldest wash, as I thoroughly scour my skin. When I make it to the room I share with Roan, the humidifier is on, and it's pumping a scent that I know well and have come to love.

It's Roan's musky and familiar scent. My body responds immediately to this concentrated incense. My nipples tighten, sweat gathers on my skin, and although I've never been that much of a sexual being, I'm soaked and achy right now.

I drop the towel, rushing to the bed, and sink into the cool sheets, a balm to my overheated flesh. Immediately, I recognize my mistake. The essence is released right next to me on the bedstand.

It's too much. I feel like... Oh hell! Oh no! I feel like I'm going to come.

I whimper, cover my head with my pillow, and feel my body shudder. I bite the pillow to stop the scream of agony from loosening from my tongue. But suddenly, the pillow and blankets are peeled from me, and my salvation stands above me.

"Please," I beg.

"Oh, my love," Roan whispers, and he strips his clothing from his body in record time. He climbs over me and cages me down, I can't stop the sigh of relief as I feel his skin against me. He rubs his cheek against my face and presses his lips gently to my soft skin. "I'm so sorry, baby."

I wrap my legs around his thighs and try to pull his hips down to my core. "No, baby. I'm not going to make love to you for the first time when you won't remember it later."

Feeling rejected, I feel tears fall. "You don't want me?"

"Shhh, I want you more and more every moment, Fred. I just won't have you like this." He brushes my damp hair back and leaves kisses everywhere from my collarbones up, causing me to be more and more frustrated.

"I want you inside me, Roan!" I beg.

"No, Freddie. If my cock touches your pussy tonight, your virginity is gone, baby, gone. It was a bad idea to get naked with you." He moves and presses his thigh to my aching cunt. It feels heavenly.

I become more and more restless. "Kiss me, kiss me please, Roan!" I cry out.

He chuckles darkly. "I've been kissing you, my love. But maybe you need a deeper kiss." He crawls down my body. "I'm going to sink my tongue in this sloppy wet pussy and give you a deeply satisfying kiss, baby. I'll keep doing it until you fall asleep."

A second later, he has me bent so my knees are pressed up to my chest. I'm on display. The first pass of his tongue through my folds makes him groan, "Fuck, baby! You're so wet, high on me, and aching for my cock. It's a dream of mine to feel you melt around me. Mmmm, this is heaven. No demon has a right to such godlike ambrosia."

I roll my hips against his face and push into his fingers, they aren't enough. I want more. "Fuck me, Roan!"

"Right? I know, baby, we both want it. But no, Freddie. I'll let them tape me up in monitors and sedate us. I'll let them poke, prod, and pollute what we have. I'll give them this noose to hang me with, where I play with your body all night long. But I'm not giving them your first time. Not *our* first time. Stop begging. I can't take your begging. Be a good girl; come on my tongue. Let me have your cum, I'll let you have mine. But in your mouth, not your pussy."

He doubles his effort, and I roll from one pinnacle to the next. I'm blinded by sensation as he pleases me. Soon, all his words are gibberish until he shakes me, and I peel my eyes open to find his gorgeous black and red eyes boring into mine.

"Can they sedate you now? I'm going to show them how I feed from you while you sleep. I won't take you in your sleep, only more of what we've been doing." He kisses my throat and scrapes his teeth against my flesh. I surrender more by turning my neck, a wordless plea for him to Claim me.

He whispers in my ear. "I'm going to come for you in your dreamscape, my love. I'll please you in all the ways I can't in this world. I can't fuck you here. I can't put a baby in you, we can't let them take our future. But I'll give you everything in our dreams."

The idea makes me feverish, not frightened. "I want your cum. Put it deep inside me."

He slaps my thigh so hard it stings, then he groans and leans down to suck hard on my clit. When he pulls up, he's shaking his head. "That's those pheromones talking. I can't do that, and if you weren't high as hell on them, you wouldn't be begging for anyone's baby batter. You're only doing it right now because you're out there in super space on demon scent." He leans down and fucks me deeply with his tongue, and when he pulls back, he draws his nose through my pussy folds. "You're fucked up on *my* demon essence, and I'm dizzy as hell on yours."

I moan and writhe below him. "I love your scent."

He chuckles. "And I love yours too. Maybe you will believe me now that we are meant for one another. When we Claim one another, those scents will mix."

"Claim me!" I pull his head down to my core and into my pussy. "Make me yours."

"When they do this to me, you're going to have your hands full. It's going to be a different conversation, entirely. I will have you dripping cum, until it's running out of you for days. But baby, let's not rush on night one."

I shudder and grab Roan by his hair and wrench him up to my lips. "Please, fuck me, mate!"

Roan kisses my brow and then addresses the room, "We need sedation. Bring in any equipment you need for me. Females only, Thomasina. Do not send in a male, or I will kill them."

I shiver at the danger in his words and raise my hips to his. His cock rubs against my pussy. "Mine!" I reach between us, and when my hands wrap around Roan's cock, his face sinks to my throat. "Roan, let me suck your cock!"

He snorts a tortured breath and then pumps into my hand experimentally a couple of times. "Tomorrow, when you aren't under the manipulation of this shit, Freddie. If you still want my dick, it's all yours."

Thomasina enters the bedroom without knocking, and a primal response bubbles up from deep inside me.

"Did she just hiss at us?" Carney asks, following Thomasina in.

"Sedate her, one of you. I can't take her feeling me up for much longer without falling victim to her seduction." Roan exhales like he's exhausted already.

Thomasina snickers, "Ben would be all for us letting nature take its course."

"This isn't nature," Roan growls, grabbing Thomasina's forearm in a brutal hold, and I make an animal sound of jealousy.

Carney comes forward with a syringe and hands it to Thomasina. "Here is Freddie's nigh' nigh' juice."

I feel a prick to my inner arm, and I reach for Roan. All there is in my world is him. It's a small and complete universe made entirely of Roan Thibodault. "Roan, come inside."

He kisses my hand, which is getting heavier and heavier. "Soon, baby. I am going to meet you in your dreamscape very soon, and I will do everything there I can't do here."

I flutter my eyelids, trying to keep them on him but they become harder and harder to focus on him. Then I'm out.

CHAPTER
NINE

I wake up slowly. For the first time in months, I feel invigorated. I reach out, wanting to touch Roan, but my hand comes in contact with hot, bare skin, and I immediately pull away.

"Oh no, Freddie Betty." He grabs my wrist and pulls me around until I'm facing him, and places a kiss on my lips. "You can't flush that pretty pink this morning after you tarted up our night, talked so dirty to me last night, and came on my face so many times."

I cover my face and try to pull away. "You're naked!"

"We're both naked! There is nothing to hide behind anymore, my love. Get used to it. Last night was a lot. I had a hard time denying you. I don't know what tonight will be like when they put me under. We're going to have to talk about it," he whispers. "Let's go get some breakfast."

I sit up and hold the sheet to my chest. "What if I can't control you?"

"You will think of something. You're the other half of me, the only one I'd ever listen to." Roan's hand caresses my back and then my hip.

I shiver. "Your touch feels like home."

"The fucking pheromones pumped all damn night." His happiness drains.

Shaking my head, I try to get him focusing back to the contentment we were just sharing. "No! Stop and think of it. If it was anyone else's scent, would it affect me? Another Incubus, like if it were Alex's or Etienne's?

He smiles a little. "It might make you a little hot, but not like you are with mine. You want me because I'm yours. You wouldn't yearn for them or their touch."

He grins and sits back, dragging me to his chest for a tight embrace. I feel like he's begging me to understand what it means, and for the first time, I do. I really do.

"You're mine," I whisper so quietly it barely escapes my breath.

He tips my chin up his way and nips my lower lip.

The door flies open, and Benjamin enters. Roan pulls the sheet up to cover me to my cheekbones and gives the man a warning look. "Last night was disappointing. It's my opinion that last night was a failure. Roan, step out."

"Not on your fucking life." My mate wraps his arms around me. "My mate is naked."

"I'm no longer convinced she's your mate. I want to see her with another subject. Maybe another pheromone mixture would have better results," Benjamin dispassionately adds.

"You were listening to our conversation a few seconds ago. You want us to be so desperate that we mate," I say with my eyes narrowed. "No. Absolutely not. I will submit to my mate tonight. We will give you results, but no one but Roan!"

I try to pull away so I can get out of bed, but Roan's arms are like iron shackles.

Benjamin nods. "I want to see a true mating and Claiming. I want it on film and with witnesses. A breeding attempt where the issue is ours."

His list of wants wind Roan tighter and tighter. I swallow my discomfort so he won't pick up on it. "Go for it. Pump it again," I cry out angrily. "We'll do it."

"No! No, baby!" Roan leans his head to my shoulder and shakes it. "I don't want to Claim you here like this. It should be special. I've waited all my life to make you mine. I need it to be special. You are too important to me."

"It will be you loving me, that is all it matters," I whisper to him.

"No, baby." He squeezes his eyes shut, not wanting to surrender our ceremony to this experiment. "We need witnesses, real ones."

"Aristade, Alexandre, Etienne...Abrielle and Terralee, maybe?" I offer.

"You don't get it, Winifred. They will be here while I fuck you. While I make love to you and while I take you for the first time in this world. They are going to watch me Claim you. I will bite you, you're going to have to bite me back. I don't know what will happen when it occurs. You're mine. I might become even more territorial than I already am." He squeezes his eyes shut and then looks at Benjamin. "Do you know what will happen to her?"

"Doesn't matter," the researcher shrugs.

"It does fucking matter!" Roan bellows.

Benjamin laughs in a sinister, low tone. "No, I mean this is my study. I decide, and I don't like this plan. I don't know if I like the direction it's going."

I watch Carney slide from the room, and when she is behind everyone, she mouths she's going to grab Aristade and Etienne.

"Fuck off, Ben," Roan snarls.

The research director laughs and heads to the door. "If that is how you want this to go down, this is going to be rushed to a quick end with you two. We can always rerun the experiment with more subjects." He nods to Thomasina. "Lock them in. Release both of their pheromones. Record everything."

Before Roan can make it to the door, Thomasina has the door closed and locked. "Fuck no! Please, no!" he screams.

"What? What's going to happen?" I ask, panic choking me as I feed off Roan's fear.

"We're fucked. I'm sorry. I pushed too hard, and now we are pawns more than ever before." He grabs his head and slides down the door. A moment later, the pheromones start pumping out of both humidifiers, but not only there, it's getting piped in through the ceiling and floor vents. "NO!" Roan stands and runs to me. "Fuck, Fred! Fuck! I'm so sorry!"

I recognize the effects immediately. I pull him down to the bed and wrap him in my embrace. "It will be okay. We will be okay."

"Babe, I would never regret being with you, but tomorrow morning, we are going to look back at this with possible awe and horror. I don't want you to hate me after this," he says as I crawl around him and straddle his lap.

The pheromones are affecting both of us. I'm ungodly wet, and he's stiff. I can't help but grind against him. "I can't. I won't hate you," I whisper against his lips.

He shakes his head. "We have to work fast. Tie me down to the bed. Gag me, muzzle me. Don't let me bite you! Keep away from my mouth."

I shake my head, push him down on his back, and crawl

up his body until I'm sitting on his face. "Make me come, Ro," I moan.

He pants below me. "Fuck! Fuck! Fuck! No, baby! I smell you, you're so ripe for me. You have to stop, Freddie. I'm going to fuck and Claim you if you don't stop! Do you want to spend the rest of your days with me in your life and around your neck like an albatross?!"

I go to get off him because some of what he is saying triggers my rational mind. But when I turn and see him lying on the bed, breathing heavily, with his engorged and beautiful cock there before me, I follow my instincts, only stopping when he scolds me.

"Stop! Fucking hell, please stop!" His voice cracks as the door rattles, and then, all of a sudden, five people enter. Etienne and Abrielle first, and they look at the pheromone steam filling the room. Aristade and Alexandre come in, with Carney following everyone. She turns and squirts what looks like quick-set epoxy and the key in the lock, preventing anyone from getting in after us and essentially stranding us inside.

The pheromones have filled my head now. I crawl back over Roan and sink my pussy over his mouth, leaning forward to suck on his gorgeous member.

"Motherfucker, Winifred Marten. If you make a lollipop out of my cock, I will bite you on the ass, and that will be only the first of many bites I give you here today." He spanks me, and I moan and grind down on his chin.

I'm not versed at all in sucking dicks, but I let my instincts take over, and Etienne chuckles. "Freddie, relax your throat and swallow him. He'll really get off on it."

I follow the directions as much as I can, and suddenly, I am on my back with Roan over me. I pull him down in a kiss and taste myself. I hear a moan that isn't mine. I look to the side to find Alexandre sucking on Carney's naked breasts. "It's normal during a Claiming for witnesses to celebrate with us." Roan chuckles as he kisses my shoulder.

I pull his hair to bare his throat and scrape my teeth against it while pushing my breasts against his chest. I want my mate to Claim me so badly.

He grabs my hands and pushes them to the bed above my head. "Don't do that! I will lose control. I'm hanging on by a thread, baby." He pets my hair back as if that will calm me.

I won't be placated, though, and using all my weight, I roll him over. While he's still surprised by my move, I grab his cock and sink down on him. I don't pause and push my way through the barrier that pronounces my innocence as gone.

He howls and moans. "No, baby. Bad move!"

A moment later, he has me flipped over, and his body is wedged between my thighs. Then he's lifting my legs over his shoulders, pushing deeper inside of me. "No! Oh, Freddie! Freddie! Freddie!" he chants.

Etienne groans, "Between the noises Fred is making and the pheromones, it's making me want to fuck all of you."

Roan growls a possessive sound.

"I won't come near your mate, asshole. I'm just saying... it's like a fucking sex carnival of both of your scents," he amends.

I'm getting so anxious and foggy, I want Roan to move. "Baby, stop moving!" He then pulls back and rams into me hard, and I revel in it, wanting more. I make a primal noise when he addresses Aristade and Etienne, though, "Please don't let me bite her like this."

Aristade stands. "Get off her then. Don't fuck her and spill inside her. If you come inside her, you will lose your ever-loving mind. At that point, none of us will get near her until after you get through Claiming her.

I snap at him when he gets near us, and Etienne gets up and comes at us from the other side. "I wouldn't have guessed Lil' Winifred Beatrice would be an animal in bed."

"Shut the fuck up," Roan barks at him.

I move my legs down his arms, sick of the interference and the delay. I pull his shoulders down and bite him until I taste blood. His hips are punching forward and pulling back without any rhythm or finesse.

Etienne grabs him by the throat and pulls Roan back. "Stop, man! You didn't want to do it like this!"

When I sit up to go to him, Aristade tackles me, laying on top of my naked body. I whine, "Fuck me, Ro. Fuck me hard. I need your Claiming bite. I need to feel you inside me. My body needs you."

Roan whimpers. "Etienne, let me go. She's my home. I knew she was." He wrenches out of Etienne's hold and fights Aristade to get back to me. "You can't deny me anymore, can you, Freddie? We belong to each other."

I nod. "I need you. You're mine. Take me, Roan. I want you deep inside me, leaving your cum running out of my cunt. I want you to live inside my virgin hole for the rest of our lives."

Alex, who has been quietly fooling around with Carney, laughs, "She certainly sounds like she belongs to him."

A second later, Roan's back inside me, sliding deep and pulling out at a torturous but jarring pounding. Soon, I'm clenching around him, and his mouth is finding its way across my flesh as he searches for the place he wants to make his.

And then it's too late to save us. Roan's demon teeth sink into the fleshy part of my upper chest, where my sternum and soft breast meet one another. I come and come and come around his cock, and he jerks inside me.

"Yes, Freddie! Suck my balls dry, my love. All my cum is for you." Then he's arranging me so I can take more of him, and he slides deeper.

The door is rattling and there is pounding from the other side.

Spots are swallowing my vision, everything is black blobs and white stars.

"Roan!" I scream, terrified.

"What's happening?!" Roan asks, panicked.

I feel fingers at my throat. "She's breathing and has a heart-beat, Ro! Calm down."

From far away, I hear Benjamin's muffled laughter and voice, "Did I forget to mention that humans can't take the bite without repercussions? She's starting the metamorphosis. We could check on her if the door wasn't locked."

I hear scuffling.

"Abby, stay with her?" Roan's voice is breaking. I feel his touch, but I don't know how I know it's him. Then he kisses me, and I fade away.

TEN

I wake slowly, feeling different. Just how different? It's a multitude of ways that start with the knowledge that Roan isn't near me, and rather than scaring me, it pisses me off. A burning anger gathers in the pit of my stomach that my Claimed mate isn't with me.

No one separates me from Roan!

I fight to open my eyes, and finally, they flutter to find the room is too bright. I try to lift my too-heavy hand. When I can't, my gaze falls to it only to find my skin color is off. My former pale tone is an ashen gray.

"You're fine, Freddie," Aristade softly says. I hear his chair scraping against the floor, and then he's beside me. "According to Thomasina, you are going through a change. They've done a ton of tests on you and Roan. You're the daughter of a demoness that Legenetics isn't used to encountering. You're a Mara; the perfect wife and mate to a Claimed Incubus."

"Where is Ro?" I ask, my voice is gravely.

"Being held in another room. They separated you as soon as they got through the door. According to Alexandre,

Roan is inconsolable." Aris sounds sad—as if he's also inconsolable.

"Where is Etienne?" My breath catches as a sharp pain pierces my side.

Aristade holds up a hand. "Don't try to move too much. You're going to be sore. Your body was literally altered during your change. It's not just your hair and skin. You will have to get used to this new figure and features."

"I can't see anything. Who put me in this nightgown?" I can only see my hand.

"Carney," Aris says as he walks up and moves the gown's sleeve. I'm thin, almost painfully.

"Why?" I whisper.

"The Mara is from the Scandinavian folklore. She is the embodiment of sleep paralysis and nightmares. You're still changing." He smiles softly. "May I check your blood pressure cuff and your monitors?"

I narrow my eyes. "Whose side are you on?"

Aris looks sad. "Roan's. Always Roan's, and by that line of thought, yours."

"What else do Maras do?" I whisper.

"They disturb the thoughts of humans, bringing on terrors. They can suffocate sleepers by manifesting on victims' chests to take their lives. The Mara is the etymological root of the word nightmare. While Incubi and Succubi feed sexually from their victims and partners, a Mara can devour one in one night." Aris quiets. "Roan doesn't know yet. They won't tell him anything. I can't see him, Alexandre can't see you. And he and I can't talk to one another."

"Will he want me as this... monster?" I would be broken without him in my life. It wouldn't be worth continuing without him, I think despondently.

"He would want you if you pulled out of this as a male demon whose main reward from the change was body odor and shit," he chuckles.

"You mean if I turned into the Golgothan?" I laugh until I cry. "You think he'd love me even if I was the shit demon of Jerusalem."

"To the ends of the Earth, Freddie." Aristade nods. "He killed Benjamin. Thomasina is running things. That Legion demon called in another one, and they are masterminding the business and research in a way Benjamin never did." He leans forward and whispers, "Carney is on our side though. Before she escaped with Etienne and Abrielle, she promised to get a message out to help."

"What does that mean?" I murmur.

"We will get you out of here and hidden away." Aris stands up and refits the blood pressure cuff.

Thomasina knocks and lets herself in. Seeing her burns away whatever drowsiness I was left feeling from the change.

"I'm going to make you miserable," I laugh at her like I'm unhinged. When it doesn't stop, I start worrying about my own well-being.

"Sure you are!" she says placatingly. Then she comes near enough to pat my leg. "But we don't know what you can do, so I'm not scared yet."

I move faster than I ever could before and wrap my fingers around her wrist and with a quick jerk, I feel a snap that makes me smirk. She howls in pain and steps back.

I bite my tongue to stop my giggling. "I guess I'm faster and stronger than you! Start a list. When I break your bones, I like it."

Thomasina dives to press a button that looks amazingly like a morphine drip. I rip out the IV that is attached to the other arm. Aristade grabs her, and I fling myself from the bed, feeling only slightly as weak as I felt earlier. I'm sure this is adrenaline, and it will drop me when it abandons me. I feel my eyes do something they never have before, and it's like I'm waking up every thought that she ever compartmentalized to function. I begin unraveling them and playing them as live ammunition back at her.

Aristade drops her into a sobbing pile and looks for something to wrap my bleeding arm. "Well, Freddie, I'm not going to lie. Your new abilities are terrifying."

A head peeks into the room, and I stalk to her. "No! Stand down!" Alex's voice calls. "This is Faith! She and a bunch of Abaddon are here to take us somewhere safe."

Faith smiles, then turns and waves behind her. When nothing happens, she sighs. "Fucking hell, Alexei, move!"

"Do you mean Alex?" I ask cautiously, moving forward.

Faith shakes her head. "No, Alexei, my bodyguard! Except he's recovering from something right now, and I'm his bodyguard for the moment."

I nod as if that makes sense. "I'm Freddie, and this is Aristade, my friend. I need to find–"

"Fred!" I hear Roan call for me. I look all over and finally set my eyes on him and push everyone out of my path to get to him. Aris is right, Roan doesn't even pause to look at the changes I've undergone. He gathers me into his arms and holds me like he can't let me go.

Faith interrupts, "We have a long way to travel and a problem to deal with." Alexei moves to her side and looks at all of us like we are possible traitors. "Aristade or Alexandre, would either of you be willing to stay behind and watch how they regather their resources here?"

I watch the brothers look at one another and have a

silent conversation. "Either we both stay or go. We stay together, though."

Faith walks in as Thomasina is struggling to stand. As the Legion researcher makes it to her feet, Faith punches her hard and knocks her out. She then turns around and takes a deep breath. "They put trackers in all of you. We need to get Freddie and Roan's out. Alexei, can you do it?"

He nods but looks reluctant. Without argument, he looks at Roan first. "Would you hold her while I remove it? I have the machine. I just have to scan for it and then make a small incision and pull it out."

Roan looks suspiciously at Alexei. "You find it, but I will remove it."

I relax against my mate at this agreement. While my tracker is being found, conversation continues about what happens next.

Aris looks unsure. "Roan and Freddie are going to remain together and safe?"

Faith nods. "We can't tell you where we are taking them right now. If you were captured and interrogated, then more than Freddie and Roan would be at risk. But soon, you will all be together. Nix wouldn't hear of it being any other way."

"Baby, lower your head. I'll get this out real quick, and then I'm going to have Alexei remove mine. We need to make tracks and get the fuck out of here." I nod and move my hair over my shoulder, and I notice that the teal is now mixed with silver.

"What the hell?" I run my fingers through my hair.

I feel a pain in my neck and try not to flinch from it.

"Give it to us!" Alexandre says, moving to us. "They will assume you are still wherever we put them."

I feel an adhesive of some sort being pressed to my skin,

then Roan's lips. He smiles against my nape. "Your scent has mixed with mine."

While Alexei works on Roan, I move to hug Aris and Alex. Faith rallies us to move faster, and then Roan, Alexei, Faith, and I are in the back of a black van with tinted windows, racing toward a municipal airfield nearby.

When we arrive, we step out, and I'm surrounded by two dozen military men. I shiver and lean back into Roan.

He wraps an arm around my shoulders and whispers in my ear, "They're Abaddon Security like Alexei. Abaddons are a type of warrior demon that is born and trained for war."

I look at Faith. "Oh no, not me. I'm a foolish human who doesn't want to face her fate just yet. I grow angrier daily over how humans and demons treat one another and have opted to save them anyway."

"I'm Winifred Marten. My friends call me Freddie," I introduce myself.

"Faith Highcraft, it's nice to meet you. I work for an Abaddon named Nix. He's Commanding Abaddon of South East Headquarters and a real pain in the ass." Her words are harsh, but she smiles fondly. Flipping her hair from one side to the other I notice she has a scar that is very visible.

Seeing where my eyes have landed, she taps the spot. "I died once, and Lucifer brought me back to life. Ruined the stories of the Fallen Angel for me completely. He's the adopted son of some of my friends now. And like you, many of my friends are humans who have gone through a Claiming. I call you converted humans."

Alexei waves us onto the private jet, which has the Nine Inch Nails logo on the side, but instead of NIN, it says NIX.

We sit next to one another, and I cling to Roan. He looks down at me. "How are you taking this, baby?"

"I'm leaving Aunt Dawn without saying goodbye," I whisper worriedly.

"We'll get a message to her somehow. We'll get something to Alexandre or Aristade, and they can let her know you're safe." He kisses my temple.

"How long until we get going?" I look around, and all of a sudden, music fills the cabin. It's Kayzo and Bad Omens' "Suffocate," and the Abaddon all seem to relax as it tunes out the sound of the engines.

The Abaddon across the aisle from Roan leans over and says to us, "We are about three-point-five hours from touching down to freedom in this jet."

I look around. "If this is a trick, I will fuck up each and every one of you. I won't risk my mate to any more Legenetics studies."

Faith laughs and comes to sit in the seat ahead of us. "You sound like Lizzy. You are going to love her and Vanth."

Roan tugs a hank of my hair and smiles as he kisses me. "These are the good guys, my love. We are almost saved."

By the time Faith commandeers the music and puts on "Beautiful Things" by Benson Boone, I am nodding off. I must sleep like the dead because the next thing I know, I wake up to the door being opened and unbearable mugginess. I fan my face with my hand and try relieving the sweat on my brow.

"You think this is bad? Wait until the summer months, Daughter of Mara," one of the Abaddon says.

We are led to the largest SUV I've ever encountered. Once I'm secured inside, Roan loads himself next to me like he would take on the world. When we arrive at the location, my eyes widen, and fear catches in my throat.

"This looks like another prison," I murmur.

Faith, who is sitting next to me, smiles sadly. "Trust me,

Freddie. This place has seen a great deal of horror. But in the years I've spent here with Nix, it's seen only good. He is a great demon, and although I didn't know they made them that way, he's single-handedly proved that there are male demons that aren't looking to hurt those weaker than them."

I nod. "I guess we can't put it off forever."

She smiles. "Kentworthy doesn't have to be your last stop. It can be where you stay until we get all your friends away from Legenetics."

Roan presses me forward. I take the first few steps with his help but then remind myself that, at this point, there is nothing worthwhile to look back to.

EPILOGUE - SIX MONTHS LATER

I run to Nix's office. "You got something?"

We haven't heard or seen anything from Alexandre, Aristade, Etienne, Carney, or Abrielle since we left. Dominique and Terralee apparently got involved with another Legenetics research study and are still with Thomasina. I was heartbroken to hear that by the time the Abaddon made it back to the Legenetics research house, it had been wiped clean. The team sent there ransacked it and came across a note that only said , *'Be with you soon.'*

"Mara?" Nix rumbles. The Abaddon seems to enjoy calling me by my new hybrid breed.

"My name is Freddie," I remind him.

"Yes, of course." He nods. "Your mate is looking for you."

"Okay... but did you find something out about anyone back home?" I look at Nix with a tilt to my head, as if seeing him at a new angle would help the puzzle that is Nix Abaddon.

"Mara—" he starts.

"Freddie," I correct.

"I have something to do in Los Angeles." He tosses his blade up into the air and catches it easily.

"So you won't be looking for my family?" I sigh, unhappily.

"Lizzy and her mate, Jonah, will be here to oversee things. She's a Celestial. I'm sure you came across something regarding it while you were rearranging the library." He smirks.

I reach out and grab the knife while it's spinning in the air. I wag my finger at him. "Pay better attention. I was reading everything I removed from the library." I point the knife at him.

"It was frightening, too. No one should have that much reading time on their hands, Mara." Nix's nostrils flare. "Gimme back my blade."

"What is the point you're making?" I ask.

"What's a Celestial?" He holds out his hand, and I turn and flip the knife up and catch it like he had been doing.

"Gods, Goddesses, and Angels reborn." I turn to him and flip the knife his way in an arc so he can catch it.

He smiles like a proud parent. "Lizzy is a Celestial. Her other side is Vanth, she's like you in many ways. Adorable."

Faith comes in through the open door. "You like the two of them because Vanth and Freddie are both bloodthirsty."

"I am not!" I argue.

"You are, though." She nods.

I turn away. "Nix, send her somewhere."

"She's staying here. You two would be lost without one another." He picks up the knife and tosses it again, and I move super fast and steal it.

I point it at him. "Finish your bad news."

"Mine first," Faith says. "The Quadrouple and Bane are coming. Why he has to leave the Fortress is beyond me. We would be fine with Crux and Tobin being here with Lizzy in charge."

"I'm going to Los Angeles, so Bane is coming here," Nix announces, and we all look at him.

Faith's shoulders fall. "I won't be held responsible."

Roan comes out of nowhere. He grabs the knife from my hand and walks it to Nix. "Enough playing with your psychotic Abaddon mentor. Time to please me like a good girl, mate."

He picks me up over his shoulder while I'm still arguing with Faith and Nix. I'm halfway down the corridor when I stop hearing them and then up the stairs to the attics, where Faith and Nix have made bedrooms from former storage.

Roan flips me onto the bed and follows me down, tickling me and only stopping when I am screeching 'mercy.'

"Did Nix tell you the other part about Jonah and Lizzy being here with us?" Roan asks, unbuttoning my shirt.

"I don't think he had time to." I push my guy up and remove my shirt and bra before placing kisses along his jaw to his mouth.

"They're going to teach us how to use dream magic and nightmares defensively and offensively. I want to know you can protect yourself if something happens to me." He groans when I slide my hand down his sweats.

"I want to know nothing will happen to you," I reply to him. "So I will do anything in this world or the dreamworld to make that happen, but Roan, I will never lose you." I tap our hearts. "I can find you anywhere, by following this. It will always lead me home."

"You're my home, too," he says, pressing his lips to mine.

"Do you think Nix has one?" I bite my lip and look up at my Claimed mate's eyes.

"Maybe. Maybe he's leaving to find his home." Roan pulls me over on top him, and I stop worrying about everyone else because my home can make me feel like there is nothing better in this world than the two of us together.

Acknowledgments

David: Thanks for the ground milk, sweaty hoodoos, being my hockey buddy, chef, shower pal, and letting me play metalcore on the Carplay even though you like pop punk. Let's re-up our marriage sub-serve this year. I can't imagine life without you, and I'm not saying that because you help me so much with my book hobby.

Thank you to Bri, Kalie, Owen, and Chanel. I appreciate you all learning to speak my screwed-up, made-up language to figure out my wants and needs. I can't express enough how touched I am when you read my text, which says, 'Blah, blah, blah—sorry I've not had coffee yet.' Yet, you know what I'm talking about.

The Good Girls authors are like a group therapy channel. I can express my author fears there, and they can assure me I'm normal.

My alpha & beta bitches, who are the best in the world. I love you all for sticking through my messy drafts and telling me the real deal of my storytelling. Raylene, Danielle, and Gloria.

My ARCholes, boy, do I love you and want to keep you. My Booksprout Babes, thanks for being there since the beginning. My ARC team, I want to make book babies with you—and I guess we are doing that already.

Marcos Nogueira, Clara Stone, and Artscandare for tirelessly bringing to life even the vaguest of my ideas. I deeply and dearly appreciate your time and patience each time we work together.

To my sister, who has read my books and thinks I'm a perv... so are you, because you've read all my books.

To my uncle, who's read none of my books and likes pie... thanks for always ensuring I'm okay.

Stay Sea Chu... I miss you so much it's like a sickness. I can't believe we are so far apart. Besties shouldn't have so many miles between each other!

I also want to say never-ending love for Zed, Ms. Peepers, Mr. Wigglesworth, Lovey Dovey, Nala Lala Lily Way, and Mitzy of Meowington.

Lastly. You, my readers... You are my rockstar sex demons. You bring me endless pleasure and pain. I love that you have taken the time to read my stories and want more.

ABOUT THE AUTHOR

Ali Lucia Sky is the author of The Powers That Be and Somnolence series. She lives in The Poconos with her husband and a house full of kitty cats. Despite her father's dismay, she's trying to seduce a squirrel to be her new friend.

She loves laughing, vegan food, and supporting her local coffee shop.

When she isn't writing or dreaming of new stories, she can be found Googling new places to travel because she suffers from wanderlust.

If you encounter her in the wild, don't be offended if she should run away. She's timid with strangers but can be plied with shiny things and pictures of your cat or dog.
    She's a weirdo like that.

Visit her website for more info and updates: https://theskywriteshere.com

Join her reader group to be the first to know all the inside scoop: https://www.facebook.com/groups/SkysSteamyBookStop

facebook.com/AliLuciaSky

instagram.com/theskywriteshere

bookbub.com/profile/ali-lucia-sky

LIST OF BOOKS BY ALI LUCIA SKY

The Powers That Be Series

The Dream Keepers

Wishcraft

Ethereal Bodies

The Powers That Be Series Bundle

Somnolence Series

RAIDEN

TRACE

JONAH

RENLEY

JUMPER

SHELBY

Legenetics: The Research Files

ROAN

The kindest way to thank an author for a good read is with a review. Please take a moment to leave your thoughts on Amazon, Bookbub, or Goodreads. That would be incredible. I always love to hear from readers. If you have anything you want to share with me, please contact me at theskywriteshere@gmail.com. *That includes any errors you've found in my novel... especially any errors you've found in my novel!*